KONG

THE 8TH WONDER OF THE WORLD™

ESCAPE FROM SKULL ISLAND

Adapted by Laura J. Burns and Melinda Metz

Based on a Motion Picture Screenplay by

Fran Walsh & Philippa Boyens & Peter Jackson

Based on a Story by

Merian C. Cooper and Edgar Wallace

SIMON AND SCHUSTER, LONDON

SKULL ISLAND

As surveyed April – September 1936

Natural Scale 1:50,000 at the equator

SOUNDINGS in FATHOMS

Mercator projection

PROLOGUE

In 1933, a ship called *The Venture* set sail from New York City. It headed toward Skull Island, deep in the Indian Ocean. In addition to the ship's crew, led by Captain Engelhorn, there was a film cast and crew onboard. The cast included Ann Darrow, a young actress eager to star in her first movie, and Bruce Baxter, a dashing actor with a less-than-dashing personality. Luckily for Ann, she got along well with the film crew and the ship's crew – especially writer Jack Driscoll. Director Carl Denham had hired Jack to write him a hit movie, and Carl was determined to make a film that would save his failing career.

But none of that mattered once the ship arrived at Skull Island. The cast and crew had no idea what danger lay ahead... danger that would be a matter of life and death...

East from Greenwich

1

Ann Darrow stared up at the huge carved stone head towering above her. The face glared down as if it wanted her and the film crew to get back on the ship and leave Skull Island – right that second.

"That's it! It scares you," coached Carl Denham, the director of the movie. "You want to scream, but your throat won't work."

Ann swallowed hard. Her throat was dry. The rocky beach and the fog that drifted in off the sea made the place feel haunted.

"Now, throw your arms across your eyes and scream," Carl instructed. "Scream, Ann. Scream for your life!"

"Ahhhhh!" she screamed. The scream sounded real because it *was* real. Ann was scared!

Suddenly, an unearthly roar echoed in the air. *Rrwowl!*

The sound was so loud that the group froze with fear.

"What was that?" Bruce asked nervously. "A bear? That was a bear, wasn't it?"

"I want to get whatever made that sound on film!" Carl exclaimed. "Come on, everybody."

Carl started across the narrow, boulder-covered strip of beach in the direction the roar had come from. The others anxiously followed.

At the top of a steep stone staircase, Carl led the group through a dark tunnel.

They came out into what was obviously a burial ground. There were tombs on either side. One of them looked like a huge mouth with jagged teeth along the top. Several of the tombs had been smashed open. Ann caught a glimpse of a mummy's hand and arm reaching out of one.

Carl was thrilled. "I *knew* Skull Island was the perfect place to make my movie!" he said. "Tons of great scary stuff!" He told Herb the cameraman to start filming.

Beyond the graves was a village of grass huts.

Preston, Carl's assistant, noticed rows of bamboo spikes surrounding the huts.

"What are they keeping in there?" he wondered aloud.

"What are they trying to keep out?" Jack answered.

All of a sudden, villagers ran out of the huts. One woman rushed out of the crowd. Her face was painted with mud. She grabbed Ann's arms with fingernails that were as sharp as claws.

"Larri yu sano korê… kweh yonê kah'weh ad larr… tôre Kông!" the woman cried. Her black eyes burned with hatred as she stared at Ann. *"Kong!"* she screeched again.

The other villagers repeated the word. *"Kong! Kong! Kong!"* they chanted, staring at Ann through narrowed eyes.

Ann struggled to escape the woman's grasp. What were they saying? What was *Kong?* And what did Kong have to do with her?

2

Kong, Kong, Kong!"

Ann was back on the ship. She was safe in her tiny cabin.

Captain Engelhorn and a group of armed sailors had rescued the film crew from the villagers. But Ann kept hearing that chant in her head, and she couldn't stop shaking.

A soft creaking sound caught Ann's attention. Her eyes moved to the doorknob, which was turning. . . .

One of the men from the village burst through the door! He slapped his hand over Ann's mouth before she could scream.

Ann twisted back and forth, but she couldn't break free.

The man dragged her out on deck. Ann prayed one of the sailors would see them. But there wasn't time. The man pulled Ann over the ship's rail – and into the icy water below.

The saltwater stung Ann's eyes as the man wrapped a rope around both of them. On the beach, a group of villagers held the other end of the rope. They began to yank on it, pulling Ann through the water. They were dragging her back to Skull Island!

As soon as she was ashore, the villagers surrounded her. They grabbed hold of her arms and rushed Ann through the graveyard and past the huts. They stopped in front of a huge, stone wall, more than two hundred feet high. Bamboo spikes and burning torches ran along the top of it. More villagers stood on the top of the wall. Some of them were beating on drums.

A woman came forward and looped a necklace around Ann's neck. It was made of thorns that were ten inches long. Ann thought she would be sick when she realized there were tiny bird skulls threaded among the thorns.

One of the men pushed Ann toward a narrow set of stone stairs that ran straight up the side of the wall. He wanted her to climb.

Ann glanced behind her, wondering if there

was any chance of escape. No. She was outnum-bered. Escape would have to wait. She started up the stairs. Her legs felt like rubber, and she feared they wouldn't carry her to the top.

Two villagers grabbed Ann the second she reached the top of the wall. They used vines to strap her into something that looked like a crane made out of tree branches tied together with more vines. Then the men pushed the crane away from the wall. Ann hung helplessly over a trench, swinging from the end of the crane.

"Kong, Kong, Kong!" the villagers shouted. Slowly, the villagers lowered the crane down. The crane was actually a bridge between the wall and what looked like an altar made of rock. Ann pulled in a long, shaky breath when her feet hit the altar. It was hard to see clearly. The smoke from the torches blurred everything around her. She frantically jerked against the vines that held her prisoner. She felt her wrists begin to bleed, but she didn't stop trying to free herself.

Just then, trees nearby in the jungle began to jerk back and forth. A flock of birds burst into the air, squawking with fear.

The earth began to shake. Something was coming... something huge!

Ann trembled as a breeze lifted the smoke. Suddenly she could see clearly. She let out a scream of terror – before her stood Kong, a twenty-five-foot-tall gorilla.

Kong leaned forward on his knuckles and stared at Ann with huge, yellow eyes. Scars crisscrossed his massive face. Then he rose to his full height and beat his chest with a deafening roar.

"Aaaahhh!" screamed Ann. She had never been so terrified. As the beast reached for her, she fainted from fear.

Bang!

A gunshot rang through the air. Kong quickly grabbed Ann and took off.

The gunshot had come from Jack and the others from **The Venture!** Jack had discovered that Ann had been kidnapped and convinced the others to help rescue her.

When they got to the altar on the island, though, it was too late.

"She's gone!" Jack said to Carl.

But Carl didn't respond. He was in shock. He had seen Kong as he escaped into the jungle.

"I only caught a glimpse – it was some kind of ape," Carl told the others.

This confused and alarmed the group. And it made Jack even more determined to find Ann.

But would they find her in time?

3

Ann's eyelids fluttered open. She wondered where she was. The scenery rushed past her. She lay on something that felt like an old base-ball glove – leathery and creased. She slid toward the edge of the surface and saw a carpet of thick, black hair.

Everything that had happened rushed back to her. She had been snatched off the rocky altar by a giant ape. And now she was a prisoner in his massive paw as he raced through the jungle.

Was this Kong? Ann wondered. *Had the villagers been calling him with their chants?*

She had no more time to think. The beast – Kong – reached a clear spot in the jungle and slammed to a stop. Ann had to grab onto his pinky finger with both arms to keep from crashing onto the large stones below.

Kong twisted his wrist. Suddenly, Ann was being held facedown over the stones. Her necklace fell off and landed on top of a pile of other necklaces made of thorns and tiny skulls. Every necklace was identical to hers. Some were almost entirely covered with green moss.

Kong has brought others here, Ann realized. *Many others.* The thought made the little hairs on the back of her neck stand on end. *What had happened to them all?*

Kong raised his hand until Ann was right in front of his face. She couldn't take her eyes away from his mouth. A long yellow tooth stuck out over his bottom lip. A river of drool slid down it.

The giant ape snarled. His hot breath blasted over Ann. It smelled like rotten meat and made her gag.

Kong opened his massive jaws. Was he going to swallow her whole?

Ann quickly looked below her. The ground was a long way down, but Ann's fear gave way to survival. There was no other way to escape. It was now or never.

Kong's grip on her loosened a little as he brought her even closer to his lips. She had to act! Ann wriggled and managed to make her way through his fingers.

She fell through the air... and landed with a *whomp!* She was on the ground among the skulls and bones. Amazingly, she staggered to her feet and ran out of the clearing and into the jungle.

Kong rose up with a roar of fury and stomped after her.

Up ahead, Ann felt the ground shake with each step Kong took. *You'll have to get your dinner somewhere else,* Ann thought, trying to push down her fear. She pumped her legs as hard as she could.

Then the ground disappeared from underneath her – and she was rolling down a hill. When she stopped, Ann scrambled to her feet.

Just then, a gunshot rang through the air. Ann was puzzled. *The villagers didn't have guns,* she thought. Then she brightened. *Those shots had to have come from Jack and Carl and the sailors.* Her friends were coming to rescue her!

With renewed hope, Ann ran even faster. But the ground continued to shake. Kong was getting closer.

Jack heard Ann's distant scream.

"Ann!" Jack yelled back. "Over here!"

Ann raced toward Jack's voice, when suddenly...

Bam! A tree landed next to her.

Ka-thunk! Another tree landed in front of her.

Kong was throwing *trees* to stop her from escaping! She raced around the trees and kept running.

Ann took a couple more steps, and then jerked to a stop just in time. She stood at the edge of a cliff.

"Jack!" Ann screeched as she turned around.

But the only one there was Kong. He loomed over her angrily.

With Kong in front of her, and the cliff behind her, there was nowhere to run.

Ann was trapped!

4

Kong raced through the jungle, clutching Ann like a rag doll. Ann flopped back and forth in his hand. She hated feeling so small and powerless.

All of a sudden, Ann heard a terrible growl – but it wasn't coming from Kong.

An instant later, a huge beast leaped at Kong. It locked its rows of jagged teeth onto the giant ape's wrist.

Ann couldn't believe what she saw in front of her. It was a real, live dinosaur!

Make that *two* real, live dinosaurs. Another one raced from the trees and grabbed onto Kong. The gorilla whipped out his arm – and slammed the first dinosaur into a tree. It crashed to the jungle floor.

Then Kong snatched the second dinosaur off his arm, wrapped his gigantic hand around the dinosaur's throat – and began to squeeze.

The dinosaur thrashed back and forth. It let out hideous wheezing cries. But it would not die.

Kong gave a grunt of frustration and dropped Ann so he could finish off the dinosaur. Stars danced in front of her eyes when she hit the ground. But she was glad the ape had let her fall. Now was the perfect time to escape!

Ann quickly looked around. She was in an ancient courtyard made up of crumbling walls and cracked, stone tiles. The narrow staircase across from her looked as if it was about

to fall apart.

Ann decided to try to get across the courtyard to that staircase. It was the only way out – and her only chance.

She began to creep across the courtyard. When she looked back, she saw that Kong had killed the dinosaur. Now he was getting ready to eat it.

Ann wished she could cover her ears to block out the hideous smacking sounds. *At least it is*

keeping Kong busy, she thought.

She started to crawl again, faster... until she saw a bunch of enormous, slimy insects swarm out of a crack in the stone tiles. They were only inches from her face!

With just a few feet to go, Ann swallowed her desire to scream and quietly rose to her feet. She scurried toward the stairway... toward freedom.

At the bottom of the staircase, she listened for Kong. But all was quiet.

That's a good sign, Ann thought.

She knew to keep moving, though. She still had to run across a clearing toward the jungle.

Halfway there, there was a loud *thud!* Kong's heavy fist slammed down on the grass in front of her.

Ann gasped and tried to run the opposite way.

Thud! Another fist blocked her way.

Ann tumbled to the ground.

Kong growled.

Get up, get up, get up! Ann ordered herself.

She leaped to her feet.

Thud! Kong's fist hit the ground again. The earth shook. Ann fell again. She felt as if she was doing her old comedy routine from the New York theater. In the act, she'd had to fall over and over again.

Kong snorted. It sounded like he was laughing at her!

Ann scrambled up. She darted around Kong's fist before the gorilla could lift it. And she ran – for about one second. Then she let her feet go out from under her, and she was on her behind on the grass.

Kong squealed with pleasure.

Ann stood up. She took half a step. Then she did another pratfall – onto her face this time. She thought that if she could keep Kong laughing, maybe he wouldn't hurt her.

She used both hands to bring herself to her feet again. Once again she fell, landing on her back.

Hwwa, hwwa, hwwa! Kong continued to laugh. He was happy. Ann knew she needed to keep him that way.

Ann tried to get up once more, but by now her whole body ached from all the falls. Her legs felt like jelly and she didn't have the energy to stand.

Kong reached out and poked her with one finger. He wanted to see more.

"Stop it," Ann said.

Kong roared and beat his chest in anger. With eyes blaring and teeth bared, Kong snatched Ann up. His fingers tightened around her body. Ann shut her eyes. She knew the end was near...

The big ape stared at her for a moment. Then, very slowly, he opened his palm and allowed Ann to slide down from it. Kong backed away and then loped off.

He had let Ann go. She was free!

5

Meanwhile, Jack and the others continued their search for Ann. They had fought off a swamp monster and a group of dinosaurs. Lives were lost, but the group pressed on. Everyone was on edge – no one knew what lurked behind each tree or rock.

As they pushed through some under-growth, Jack suddenly signaled the group to freeze. They listened and heard footsteps approaching. Something was headed right toward them!

Could it be Ann? Jack wondered.

But before he could say a word, one of the men fired a shot!

"No!" Jack cried.

Then came the *thunk!* of a falling body.

The group exchanged looks and went to investigate. They discovered a large, flightless bird.

Jack gave a sigh of relief. And the search continued...

In another part of the jungle, Ann hurried along. Now that Kong had left her alone, she just had to find Jack and the others.

She spotted a plume of smoke in the distance and headed that way.

The smoke must come from the village, she thought. She knew she could find her way to the beach from there. *And once I get to the beach, I will swim to the ship if I have to!*

Ann was about to step into a clearing when she saw another dinosaur – a different kind from the ones that had attacked Kong. This dinosaur was smaller, about eight feet tall.

Ann froze. *Did the creature see her?* She could see its nostrils twitching. *Did it smell her?*

She didn't want to find out. Ann turned to run – and saw another dinosaur behind her!

This one looked right at her.

Ann dashed deeper into the jungle. She could hear the two dinosaurs pounding after her.

Then Ann had an idea. She dropped to the ground and slithered between the roots of an enormous tree for protection.

The dinosaurs tried to squeeze their snouts between the roots. Their hot breath surrounded her.

Weeargh! One of the dinosaurs gave a squeal of surprise as it was lifted straight off the ground. Its taloned feet thrashed about in midair. Ann couldn't see what new creature was attacking the dinosaur. Almost immediately, the *other* dinosaur turned and fled.

But Ann didn't move. She wasn't leaving her safe cave of roots.

She changed her plan instantly, though, when a long, hairy leg brushed across her back. The long, hairy leg was attached to a giant, hairy spider!

"Ahhhh!" Ann screamed. She scrambled away from the nest of tree roots… and ran right in front of a Vastatosaurus rex!

The V. rex towered over her with the smaller dinosaur in its jaws. The V. rex was the creature that had killed the other dinosaur! As soon as it saw Ann, the V. rex dropped its prey and took off after her instead.

Ann ran, but the V. rex was a lot faster than she was. She spotted a fallen tree sticking over the edge of a cliff. She was pretty sure it would hold her weight – but it definitely wouldn't hold the dinosaur. Ann crept out on the moss-covered log as far as she could go.

Don't look down, she told herself.

The ground was a long way off – at least fifteen feet.

The V. rex watched her as she crept out over the cliff. Then it shoved the log with one of its claws. The big log teetered, and Ann held on with all her might.

Again the V. rex pushed the log. It bounced up and down like a seesaw. Then it tottered over the edge of the cliff! Ann landed hard, with the log on top of her!

Bearing down on her, the V. rex prepared for its final lunge, its huge jaws wide open.

At that moment, Kong arrived!

The giant ape and the V. rex circled each other. In a flash, Kong was on top of the V. rex, pounding his fists onto its body until it fell.

Satisfied, Kong swept Ann up in his hand. But the fight wasn't over. Two more V. rexes appeared, ready to fight. And the first V. rex staggered back to its feet.

Ann's heart stopped for a moment. *No one could battle three V. rexes at one time and win. Not even Kong,* she thought.

But Kong didn't turn and run. After putting Ann down, he attacked those dinosaurs in a breathtaking battle. Kong pulled a large, jagged tree out of the ground and rammed it into the first V. rex's open mouth.

Then the second V. rex attacked and set its teeth around Kong's throat. Kong got it into a headlock and flipped it over his shoulder.

Ann could barely stay out of the way, let alone watch. She darted beneath the beasts' legs.

Suddenly, Ann felt hot breath against her back – then she was snatched up into the jaws of the third V. rex!

She was sure that she was going to die. But Kong came to her rescue again. He grabbed the V. rex's upper jaw with one hand. He snatched the dinosaur's lower jaw with his other hand. Then Kong used all his strength to rip open its jaws.

Ann tumbled from the V. rex's mouth. The dinosaur fell to the ground with an ear-splitting groan.

Ann stared up at Kong. New cuts covered his face. A ragged patch of skin and fur hung from his throat. *He got hurt that badly to save me,* she realized.

Kong beat on his chest with both fists. He gave a roar of pride.

But the sound of gunshots interrupted his victory celebration. He snatched Ann up and raced through the jungle.

The gunshots had come from the rescue party. They were not coping so well. After battling giant insects, the mood had definitely changed . . . for the worse.

"It's useless," said Captain Engelhorn, ready to give up.

But Jack was determined to find Ann.

"Then I'll be seeing you," said Jack.

"Don't be a fool!" said Engelhorn. "She's dead."

Jack refused to listen. He told the others to keep the bridge down so he and Ann could get back across. Then he set off on his own. He had to find Ann – no matter what.

6

With Ann in hand, Kong ran through the jungle, heading toward a tall mountain. Ann noticed that the big gorilla held her more gently now. He didn't want to hurt her anymore.

They came to a ditch in the ground. Kong jumped across, reaching out for a thick vine on the other side. The vine came loose in his giant hand, and Kong fell backward. Ann landed safely on top of his chest.

Immediately, Kong got back to his feet, growling. He put Ann on the ground behind him, as if to protect her.

Ann peered around Kong's huge body. A face stared back at her from behind the vines. It was a carving in the stone wall of the ditch. It had been hidden by the vines until Kong accidentally pulled them down.

Kong snarled, challenging the face. He thought it was real.

"It's all right," Ann said. "It's okay."

She felt sorry for the big ape. *His life must be very hard,* she thought. *Even though he is so strong, every day is a battle for survival. That's why he expects to do battle with this stone face.*

Ann hurried over to the wall and pulled away the vines to reveal the entire carving – an ancient, life-size statue of a sitting gorilla. A giant gorilla, just like Kong.

"Look, it's you," she said, trying to make him understand. "Kong. See? You. Kong. This is you."

Kong stared at the stone gorilla. Then he looked down at his big hands. He seemed to understand that the statue looked like him.

Kong picked Ann up and turned away. He headed for the mountain and began to climb. Ann clung to his big fingers and didn't look down. She couldn't tell how high up they were, but she knew it had to be at least a thousand feet.

Suddenly, a bat swooped through the air.

Just like all the other creatures on this island, the bat was gigantic. It was bony and scary-looking, with a face like a reptile and long, sharp teeth. It let out a screech and dived at Ann with its sharp claws outstretched.

Kong pulled Ann in against his hairy chest to protect her. Angry, the bat whirled away.

Then Kong climbed all the way to the top of the mountain. He set Ann down on a rocky ledge that jutted out over the jungle far below. Thick green vines grew along the cliff, trailing over the edge. At the back of the ledge was the entrance to a cave – Kong's home.

Kong went to the edge of the cliff and sat down with his back to Ann. He had seemed unhappy ever since they had seen the carving in the jungle.

Ann stepped into the dark cave. A skeleton lay inside, the bones gleaming white. There was a giant skull and a huge rib cage. Ann caught her breath. These were the remains of a mighty gorilla, maybe Kong's mother or father.

Had Kong lost his whole family? she wondered. *Is he the last of his kind? No wonder he looks so sad.*

Deeper inside the big cave, Ann heard a strange rustling noise. Then, suddenly, glaring red eyes were racing toward her. It was another giant bat!

Ann ran from the cave and hid behind one of Kong's legs. The bat flew off.

Now Ann was sure that Kong would protect her from anything else that attacked. Somehow she had made friends with this big ape.

"Kong?" she said.

The gorilla turned away from her.

Ann did a little tap dance, trying to cheer him up. He had laughed at her fake falls in the jungle. She thought he might like dancing, too. But Kong still didn't look at her. She picked up a stone from the ground and rolled it up and down her arm, trying to amuse him. Yet Kong didn't react.

"Look at me," Ann begged, tugging on one huge finger. "Look at me."

Finally, he did. It almost looked as if there were tears in his big eyes.

Ann gazed out at the sprawling jungle. The sun was going down, and the sky had turned the color of fire.

"It's beautiful," Ann said.

Kong gave a soft growl.

"Beautiful," Ann repeated. She put her hand over her heart. *"Beau-ti-ful."*

Kong watched her closely. Ann got the feeling that he could tell what she meant. He put his big hand down on the ground beside her and unfurled his fingers. It was an invitation. Ann climbed into his hand and let him pick her up. He studied her face and touched her blond hair with one huge finger.

Ann smiled. She wasn't afraid of Kong anymore.

7

That night, Jack crawled out from behind a huge rock on the mountain. He could see the massive shape of Kong sleeping in the cave. Jack could make out bats fluttering about in back of the cave. He scanned the cave for any sign of Ann, but he didn't see her.

He'd have to go into the cave... toward Kong.

As Jack slowly entered, he could see Kong's giant shoulders heaving with each breath he took. Jack crept past Kong's feet – and gasped.

Ann was asleep in Kong's hand!

A bat stirred, and Ann's eyes opened. She looked around and saw Jack.

Jack put his finger to his lips to remind Ann to be quiet. Ann nodded. The last thing she wanted to do was wake Kong up.

Ann slowly sat up. She inched her way along Kong's hand. Jack crept toward her. He reached for her hand. She reached for his. Their fingers touched... and a huge bat shrieked and headed straight toward them!

Kong's eyes snapped open. He took one

look at Jack and the bat, and then his fingers closed around Ann. He pulled her into the air as he rolled to his feet.

Ann cried out in frustration. She knew Kong was only trying to keep her safe. He did not understand that Jack was her friend.

Kong snarled. More large bats flew out of the cave, but Kong kept his eyes on Jack. Ann could tell that he was about to attack.

"Jack, run!" she cried.

Kong swatted at Jack, but Jack leaped out of the way. Ann struggled in the big ape's hand.

"No! Kong, no!" she called.

It was useless. He didn't understand her. Kong put Ann down on a ledge above the cave. He turned to Jack, and raised his foot.

Bam!

Kong's huge foot pummeled into the ground.

But Jack had dived out of the way just in time. With a furious roar, Kong lifted his foot again, ready to squash Jack like a bug.

Jack looked up in shock as Kong reared above him.

Was this the end for Jack?

8

"*Aaahhhh!*" Ann cried out in pain. A bat's sharp claw gripped her arm. Ann yanked herself away from the horrible creature. It shrieked at her, its foul-smelling breath hitting her in the face.

Suddenly, another bat joined in. It swooped toward Ann, reaching out to grab her with its talons. She was stuck on the ledge. There was nowhere to hide from the attack.

Kong turned and roared with anger. He charged at the bats. He pulled Ann off the ledge and held her against his chest as the bats tried to grab her.

Ann looked around frantically for Jack. She was relieved to see him in the cave – and still alive!

More and more bats attacked. They swarmed around Ann and Kong like angry wasps. Kong roared and swatted at them with his free hand, but there were too many to fight.

So he placed Ann on the ground and attacked the bats with both hands. With every swat, Kong knocked down at least two bats. But more kept coming.

While Kong was busy fighting the bats, Jack ran to Ann. He grabbed her hand and began to run toward the edge of the cliff. But where could they go? Kong's lair was at the top of the high mountain.

Jack took hold of a thick vine, testing its strength.

"This way!" Jack said to Ann, urgently.

Ann couldn't believe it – he wanted to climb down the sheer cliff face on a vine! *What if the vine snapped – or if it was too short to reach to the bottom?* she worried.

Kong roared and slapped another bat out of the air.

Ann bit her lip. She knew that if they stayed up here, Kong would kill Jack for sure. There was no other way down. They had to risk it.

Jack pulled Ann to him and clambered over the edge of the cliff.

As Kong battled the bats, Jack moved quickly down the vine.

Soon they were twenty feet below the cliff. Then thirty. Forty. Fifty. The ground was in view!

A wild hope filled Ann's mind. *Had they escaped for good?*

Suddenly, the vine lurched upward. Ann gasped. She and Jack looked up – and saw Kong peering down at them from the top of the cliff. He was pulling the vine back up!

When they were almost back at the top of the cliff, a few bats hovered around them. One of them dived at Ann and Jack. It missed, and then wheeled around and dived again. It clawed at Jack's head.

Then Jack had an idea. He let go of the vine with one hand and grabbed onto the bat's ankle.

"Hang on to me!" he called to Ann.

She held on as tight as she could. Jack grabbed the bat's other ankle with his other hand. The bat beat its wings, trying to stay in the air. But Ann and Jack were too heavy. Their weight pulled the bat downward – fast!

Kong roared up above, but he couldn't reach them now.

The bat wobbled. It couldn't hold them up much longer. Ann glanced down. Far below them was a swiftly flowing river.

Jack let go of the bat. Ann screamed as she and Jack tumbled through the air.

Splash!

The water closed over their heads when they hit the river.

Jack and Ann swam to the surface. They had escaped!

9

Jack and Ann hauled themselves up onto the muddy bank of the river.

"Did he follow us?" Ann asked Jack.

"I think it's safe to assume that he will," Jack replied.

"Thank you," Ann said to Jack.

"For what?" asked Jack.

"Coming back," Ann said with a smile.

Just then, they heard a roar echoing through the jungle.

"Let's go!" Jack exclaimed, and they immediately took off.

They had to reach the village before Kong found them. Then they could row the lifeboats back out to the ship.

Thonk! Thonk! Thonk! The ground shook

as Kong grew closer.

Jack and Ann ran faster. Could they get to the village before the ape caught up to them?

They ran and ran until they saw the huge wall of the village. They were almost there! All they had to do was make it to the bridge that spanned the trench between them and the wall...

Jack stopped in his tracks. Ann tumbled into him. He was staring up at the wall, frowning. Ann followed his gaze. The bridge was *up!*

Oh, no! Ann thought. The bridge was the only way across the deep trench.

"Drop the bridge!" Jack yelled.

But nobody answered.

Jack tried again. "Carl?"

Ann looked to the top of the wall. No one was there. "Help us! Please! Anyone!" she cried in desperation.

A loud roar from Kong was the only answer. Trees in the jungle behind them crashed to the ground as the mighty ape smashed through the forest. He would reach them any second.

The bridge stayed up. It seemed that their friends and the crew had abandoned Ann and Jack!

Just then, Kong appeared from the jungle.
He took one look at Ann and charged forward.
Crash!

54

The bridge slammed down! Ann and Jack sprinted across it. Up ahead, there was a hole that had been blasted in the tall bamboo gate. Jack grabbed Ann's hand and pulled her through it, into the village. It was deserted.

Jack and Ann were confused. Who had let the bridge down?

Carl stepped out from behind a straw hut. He didn't look at Jack or Ann. His eyes were fixed on the gate. Kong was smashing it from outside, pounding his giant fists against the bamboo posts.

In no time, Kong had smashed through the gate!

Ann looked up at Kong, and he gazed right back at her. He reached out for her.

Just then, Carl yelled, "Bring him down! Do it!"

"Now!" yelled Captain Engelhorn.

On that command, a bunch of sailors jumped out from behind the huts. They threw grappling hooks at Kong. The metal bit into his fur, and he bellowed in pain.

"No!" Ann cried.

"Are you out of your mind, Carl?" Jack yelled in disbelief.

More sailors appeared on top of the wall. They threw a huge net over Kong's head. The big gorilla fell to the ground, trapped in the netting.

Captain Engelhorn smashed a bottle of chloroform right near Kong's face, trying to knock him out. But it didn't work.

"No!" Ann rushed toward the gorilla that had saved her so many times. "Please don't do this to him!"

Jack pulled her back. "Ann, he'll kill you."

"No, he won't!" she said, defiantly.

Ann broke away from Jack and rushed at Engelhorn. She grabbed his arm before he could throw another chloroform bottle.

"Stop it!" Ann cried. "You're killing him!"

"Get her out of here!" yelled Engelhorn. "Get her out of his sight!"

Jack pulled Ann toward the tunnel that led down to the beach.

When Kong saw that Ann was being taken away, he exploded with anger. He jumped to

his feet and tore the net to pieces. He stormed through the village, trampling huts and swatting down the sailors who tried to stop him.

Jack dragged Ann to the lifeboats that waited on the beach.

"Get in the boat!" Jack told her. He tried to lift her onboard, but Ann jerked away from him.

"No! It's me Kong wants," she said. "I can stop him from attacking everyone. Let me go to him!"

Kong's roar echoed through the tunnel. He thundered toward the beach.

Jack pushed Ann into the boat. Carl and the sailors jumped into the other boats. They rowed as fast as they could toward the ship. Some of the men shot at Kong as he followed them. He waded out into the water. The bullets didn't bother him. He wanted Ann.

Kong smashed his fist down on one of the boats. It splintered in half and sank. Ann gasped, terrified. She knew Kong wouldn't stop until he thought she was safe.

Ann heard a sound in the boat behind her. Captain Engelhorn had a harpoon gun. He was getting ready to shoot a metal spear at Kong.

Ann cried out in horror. *He doesn't deserve to die!* she thought. *He is only trying to protect me!*

Ann stared at Kong. He gazed back at her.

"Go back!" she called to him. How could she make him understand?

Engelhorn fired the harpoon. It hit Kong in the knee. The huge ape roared in pain and sank down into the water.

Engelhorn prepared to shoot another harpoon.

"No!" Ann sobbed. "Leave him alone!"

"Wait!" yelled Carl.

He climbed onto a rock in the water near Kong and threw another bottle of chloroform. It smashed against the gorilla's face. Kong choked. This time the gas had gotten to him.

Kong crawled toward Ann, reaching for her. His eyes never left hers as his gigantic body collapsed into the ocean.

The crew all cheered. Ann let out a final cry and buried her face in her hands.

The mighty ape had finally lost a fight. Kong was now a captive.